Halloween
Helpers

Halloween Helpers

Judy Delton

Illustrated by Alan Tiegreen

A YEARLING BOOK

Published by
Bantam Doubleday Dell Books for Young Readers
a division of
Bantam Doubleday Dell Publishing Group, Inc.
1540 Broadway
New York, New York 10036

The trademarks Yearling® and Dell® are registered in the U.S. Patent and Trademark Office and in other countries.

ISBN: 0-440-41330-3

Printed in the United States of America

October 1997

10 9 8 7 6 5 4 3 2

CWO

For Amy La Roche:
It's not nearly as much fun without you.

Contents

CHAPTER 1

Missing: One Pee Wee Scout Leader

"**H**alloween is my favorite holiday in the whole world," said Sonny Stone.

"Mine too," said Tim Noon.

"I think they should take all the other holidays like Veterans Day and Easter and Christmas and turn them into Halloween," said Tracy Barnes. "Then we could go trick-or-treating

1

about ten times a year, instead of just once."

Rachel Meyers looked at Tracy.

"That's really dumb," she said. "Tricks or treats on *Christmas*? And Hannukah and the Fourth of July? What about Frosty the Snowman and the Easter parade and hiding eggs and all that stuff?"

"One Halloween is enough," said Molly Duff. "If it's a good one."

The rest of the Pee Wee Scouts agreed. They were sitting in Mrs. Peters's backyard waiting for their troop meeting to begin. Mrs. Peters was their troop leader. The thirteen Scouts met in her basement every Tuesday afternoon. But today she had not arrived, and her house was locked.

It was October and there was a chill in the air, even though the sun was shining. Winter was on the way. But first, of course, there was Halloween.

"I'm going to get the scariest costume ever," said Sonny. "I'm going to scare all of you really bad."

"Ha," laughed Roger. "You'll scare yourself, Stone, more than anybody. You're a scaredy baby about everything."

"He is, you know," said Mary Beth Kelly. She was Molly's best friend. "My grandma would say he's scared of his own shadow."

"It isn't his fault. His mom babies him," said Molly.

Sonny's mother was the assistant Scout leader. And she did baby Sonny, even though she had adopted baby twins who were a lot younger than he was.

Sonny was chasing Roger around the picnic table with an angleworm. He was trying to put it down Roger's shirt, but Roger was too fast for him.

"I hope Mrs. Peters has a big Halloween party planned for us," said Lisa Ronning. "The Pee Wee party is always the most fun."

"Unless we have go to the nursing home and do good deeds again," groaned Roger.

"That was one of the best parties ever!" said Lisa.

"Roger didn't like it because when we bobbed for apples he fell in the tub up to his neck!" said Patty Baker.

All the Pee Wees remembered and be-

gan to laugh. Roger turned bright red. He liked to laugh at others, but he hated it when other people laughed at him.

"Where is Mrs. Peters?" asked Kenny Baker, who was Patty's twin brother. "She's late."

"Mrs. Peters is never late," said Molly to Mary Beth. "I wonder where she is."

There was no sign of Mrs. Peters. Or Mr. Peters. Or even Mrs. Stone, who always served the cupcakes at meetings.

"Maybe she's playing a joke on us," said Tim. "Like April Fools'."

"It's not April," scoffed Rachel.

Some of the Pee Wees were getting restless. They were what Molly's mother would call "acting up."

Rachel stood up and clapped her hands the way Mrs. Peters always did. When Mrs. Peters clapped her hands everyone was quiet. Rachel clapped her hands again. It was still noisy. *"Quiet!"* Rachel shouted.

The Pee Wees stopped acting up and looked at her.

"Since Mrs. Peters and Mrs. Stone are not here, I am next in line to be in charge," she said.

Roger snorted and asked, "Who died and made you troop leader?"

Rachel glared at him and said, "I'm the oldest. Sit down and be quiet."

Roger said, "Make me," but he sat down anyway. So did everyone else.

"We'll begin our meeting by singing our Pee Wee song," said Rachel.

The Pee Wees sang. A little off key, but they sang. When they finished, Rachel said, "Now we'll tell our good deeds for the week."

"Good," said Tracy. "Then we won't have to do it when Mrs. Peters gets here. We can get right to the cupcakes."

"And our new badge," said Molly.

Some of the good deeds people were describing were not real. Molly could tell. She was sure that Roger had not saved three children from a burning building. Mrs. Peters would not have let that get by. But then, Rachel probably didn't want to argue with Roger. She had no proof that he *hadn't* done it.

After fifteen minutes of good deeds, Molly began to worry about Mrs. Peters. Rat's knees, where was she? Things were all backward. Adults usually worry about children when they're late. Children aren't supposed to worry about adults.

Mary Beth looked at her watch.

"Maybe some aliens kidnapped her and took her to another planet," said Roger. The boys made alien noises and rocket motions in the air.

Molly was positive it wasn't aliens. But something was wrong, that was for sure. Mrs. Peters would not leave thirteen Pee Wees at her house unattended. Rachel was trying to carry on with the meeting, but she looked worried. And the Pee Wees were not going to mind Rachel much longer. Soon Roger would rebel, and then what would happen?

CHAPTER 2

A Tight Ship

"What are we going to do?" whispered Mary Beth to Molly.

"Maybe we should call the police," said Molly.

Lisa shook her head. "You have to be missing for twenty-four hours before they'll do anything," she said. "I heard it on *Emergency 911*."

"I think we should sit tight," said Kenny. "That's what my mom says when there's a problem. Sit tight."

"How do you do that, Baker?" roared Roger. He put his arms around his own body and tried to hug himself tightly. "Hey," he called. "I'm sitting tight. Look at me, you guys!"

Soon the other Pee Wees began to stretch into strange positions in order to sit tight.

But Molly did not think it was a laughing matter. It could be serious. Who had stolen their leader, and why?

Just when Molly was thinking about running out in the street and breaking the glass box that said BREAK IN CASE OF EMERGENCY, one of Mrs. Peters's neighbors came running around the side of the house toward them. The Pee Wees recognized Mrs. Wood. She had a man with her. A man who was not a neighbor. The man walked stiff and straight as if he was used to marching. Even though he had a regular suit on, he looked as if he were wearing a uniform, thought Molly.

"This is Mrs. Peters's cousin," said Mrs. Wood, who was slightly out of breath from running. "He has the key to the house and will carry on for Mrs. Peters today."

The neighbor left, and the man gave a slight bow. Then he raised his hand to his forehead and saluted the Pee Wees.

"My name is Captain Spencer," he said. "I have some good news for Troop 23, and some bad news."

The Pee Wees stopped what they were doing and sat, frozen.

"The bad news is that Mrs. Peters was

suddenly called away because of a family emergency. The good news is that I have been drafted as Scout leader until she returns. I am Mrs. Peters's second cousin once removed, recently honorably discharged from the army."

"Why does he talk so funny?" whispered Patty to Lisa.

"It's army talk," said Kenny.

Sonny and Roger began shooting make-believe guns at each other.

"Mrs. Peters wouldn't let them do that," said Mary Beth to Molly.

Without warning, the captain shouted, "Attention! There will be no talking while I am talking. I run a tight ship here."

The Pee Wees all jumped. Captain Spencer was scary. And what was this

talk about a tight ship? *Tight* was a popular word today. *Sit tight. Tight ship.*

Captain Spencer took a key out of his pocket and said, "Fall in."

He marched to the Peterses' back door and unlocked it. When he turned around, the Pee Wees had not fallen in. They had not moved.

"Fall in, I said."

"Fall in what?" asked Roger.

"A puddle? A hole?" giggled Sonny, who suddenly seemed very brave.

"Fall in rank!" shouted Captain Spencer.

No one knew what rank was. Molly felt like crying. How could Mrs. Peters do this to them, and for how long?

"Line up!" boomed the general.

The Pee Wees never lined up. They usually just ran into the house and down the basement stairs. But the captain lined them up, a line of boys and a line of girls. "Stomach in, chest out," he said. "Breathe deeply, forward march."

The Pee Wees marched. One, two, three, and down the steps.

The only one who didn't march was Jody George, because of his wheelchair.

When everyone was downstairs, Captain Spencer said, "I can see there is a lot of work to be done to get you in shape. Scouts are like soldiers. They need rules and order."

"Scouts are helpers, Scouts have fun!" shouted Tim. "That's what our song says."

Captain Spencer sighed. "Life is not fun and games," he said. "Life is work. Scouting prepares us for life. It gives us rules and regulations to live by."

"It gives us new badges," said Sonny. "And where's my mother? She's assistant Scout leader."

"Mrs. Stone has had an emergency of her own," said the captain. "One of her youngsters swallowed a foreign object and had to have it removed."

All the Pee Wees looked alarmed, including Sonny. What was a foreign object, and how could one of the twins have swallowed it? Molly knew *foreign* meant another country. Could one of the twins have swallowed a country?

She asked Rachel because Rachel usually knew everything the other Scouts did not.

But Rachel didn't know. She did know it was not a country. "It must be something from Germany," she said.

"Like part of a cuckoo clock. We have a cuckoo clock from Germany. Maybe he swallowed the cuckoo bird."

"Sauerkraut is German," said Tracy. "Maybe that's what he swallowed."

The captain was now busy making name tags for everyone. The tags had only the last names of the Pee Wees on them. He pinned one to each Pee Wee's collar or T-shirt.

"We know our names," said Kevin.

"But I don't," said Captain Spencer. "Now then, Duff, could you stand, please?"

The Pee Wees giggled. The captain frowned. Duff stood.

"Could you please tell me the operational procedure?" the captain asked.

Everyone stared. This man used big

words. He was worse than any teacher. Didn't he know anything about kids?

All of a sudden Sonny burst into tears. "I don't want an operation! I want my mother!"

Some of the other Pee Wees began to cry too.

"I want Mrs. Peters," said Tim.

Captain Spencer looked puzzled. Molly was sure he was not used to being around children. He patted the crying Pee Wees on the shoulder, but it didn't seem as if his heart was in it. Sonny threw his arms around the captain's neck and sobbed.

"Now, now, Stone," said the captain. "No need to panic. I just want to find out your *modus operandi* here."

Now even more Pee Wees wept. Ra-

chel finally went up to Captain Spencer and tugged at his sleeve.

"Sir," she said. "You need to use words we understand."

The captain frowned, as if that was something he would have a hard time doing.

"What do you do at your meetings?" he finally asked.

Well. Now he was making some sense.

"We eat cupcakes," called Lisa.

"We sing," said Tracy.

"We tell about our good deeds," said Jody.

"We get badges," said Mary Beth.

"We have fun and help others," said Molly.

"Just like the army!" said Captain Spencer. "Just like the army!"

CHAPTER 3

Good-bye, Mrs. Peters; Hello, Army Life!

Things went a little more smoothly after that. But Roger and Sonny got silly and could not settle down. And even though Captain Spencer was tough and called them White and Stone, they wouldn't listen. They weren't scared anymore.

"He could throw you in the brig,"

whispered Rachel. "Or put you on KP duty. I saw it in a movie once."

"I'd go AWOL," laughed Roger.

The meeting was not off to a good start. There was no Mrs. Peters. And there were no cupcakes or treats. And worst of all, there was no mention by Captain Spencer of badges *or* Halloween!

"This guy probably doesn't even celebrate Halloween," grumbled Kevin to Molly.

Not celebrate Halloween? That was almost un-American! Anyone in the army should be more patriotic, thought Molly.

"We can't earn a badge without Mrs. Peters," sighed Tracy. "All our badges come from Mrs. Peters. No stranger can do that."

Even Jody was forced to admit that

the scariest thing about Halloween this year was the absence of their Scout leader.

"We didn't appreciate her when we had her," he said wisely.

After talking about how to survive in the woods by boiling bark and cooking meat over an open campfire, Captain Spencer showed them how to tie a rope into fourteen different kinds of knots.

"Bor-ing," said Lisa. "Why do we have to know this dumb stuff?"

"Captain Spencer must think that's what Scouts do," said Mary Beth. "Army stuff."

After that, Captain Spencer passed out some sheets of paper with words to circle and pictures to color. He put some crayons on the table, told them to color inside the lines, and sat down at Mr. Peters's workbench to read an army manual.

"This is busywork," said Rachel. "It's kindergarten stuff!"

When the Scouts were finished, they were bored and restless. Roger made mouth noises and threw crayons. The captain asked him to step into the laundry room. But when he came out, Roger was laughing and was just as annoying as ever.

"Mrs. Peters knew how to handle Roger," said Mary Beth. "Not many people do."

Molly didn't like the word *knew*. It implied that Mrs. Peters was gone for good. And that this man was here to stay.

"Captain Spencer is going to have trouble with Roger and Sonny," said Rachel.

Roger and Sonny did seem to be out of control. They were making paper airplanes out of their busywork and sailing them over the captain's head. Captain Spencer's face turned red, and finally he said, "At ease, men. Class dismissed."

Even though it was early and there had been no treats, Captain Spencer ended the meeting. Thirteen very sad Pee Wees marched in two straight lines up the basement steps and out the back door.

All the way home the Pee Wees talked about their bad luck.

"It isn't fair," said Rachel.

"How could Mrs. Peters desert us?" said Mary Beth.

"What kind of family emergency could there be?" asked Molly.

"Maybe Mrs. Peters is sick," said Lisa.

"Maybe she's going to have another baby," said Patty wisely.

Molly thought about that. There could be worse things. Another baby would keep Mrs. Peters busy, but she could still be Scout leader. Mrs. Peters's first baby, Nick, had not stood in the way of the Pee Wee Scouts.

Ashley shook her head. "Having a baby is not a family emergency," she said.

"Maybe Mr. Peters got transferred to another city," said Tim.

Jody shook his head. "They wouldn't move that fast," he said. "Without saying good-bye."

Jody was right, thought Molly. Mrs.

Peters would be back. It had to be a temporary emergency. Their leader would not abandon them.

When Molly got home, all her questions were answered. Her mother met her at the door and said, "I just heard the news. Mrs. Peters had to rush to Milwaukee to care for her mother, who is ill. How was the new leader?"

New leader? Had Molly heard her mother right? Surely Captain Spencer could not be a genuine troop leader, the real thing, a replacement for their beloved Mrs. Peters!

"But Mrs. Peters has to come back!" cried Molly.

"Oh, yes," said Mrs. Duff. "I'm sure she'll be back."

But her mother's words did not feel sure at all. They felt as if maybe Mrs.

Peters would be back and maybe she wouldn't. If she really was coming back, Mrs. Duff would say, "Of course she will. She will be back next Tuesday."

Instead, Mrs. Duff said, "Her mother is old, and there's no one else to take care of her. It's hard to say just when she'll be well enough for Mrs. Peters to come home. She took baby Nick with her."

Took baby Nick? Why didn't she leave him with Mr. Peters? Why didn't she get a baby-sitter?

Molly knew why. Because Mrs. Peters was going to stay a long time. After all, she couldn't leave her poor, sick mother alone in another city. And she could not leave baby Nick with his dad because his dad had to go to work. This meant only one thing: Mrs. Peters was not going to welcome the Pee Wees in her basement next Tuesday. Or any other Tuesday.

There would be no Halloween party.

There would be no new badges.

There would be only tying knots and coloring pictures.

It was good-bye, Mrs. Peters. And hello, Captain Spencer!

CHAPTER 4

Welcome,
Ms. Bubble Gum

Molly called Mary Beth and Rachel and some of the other Scouts and told them the bad news.

"It won't be any fun waiting for Tuesdays anymore," said Mary Beth.

Molly agreed. She used to count the days and hours till Pee Wee time. Now it didn't matter. There was a hole in her life where the fun used to be.

To make matters worse, the Pee Wees

were not going to meet at Mrs. Peters's house anymore. They were going to meet at a room in the town hall. There would be no smell of baking cupcakes. Just a cold, dusty room with city maps on the wall and posters that said MOONY FOR MAYOR.

On Tuesday, the Pee Wees trudged slowly up the steps of the town hall and into their new meeting room.

"This feels like the principal's office at school," said Sonny.

"He should know, he gets sent there often enough," said Ashley.

"Maybe Roger won't be here today," said Molly.

But he was. The rest of the Pee Wees could hear him coming even though he was way down the hall. When Roger was nearby, thought Molly, you could feel it in your skin. It felt goose-bumpy even before you could see him in person.

"Where's that stupid Scout leader?" laughed Roger.

None of the Pee Wees ever called an adult stupid. It was definitely not a nice thing to do. But there was no one there to stop Roger from doing it.

Rachel glared at him. "You're the stupid Pee Wee Scout," she said.

Now the whole troop was shocked! Rat's knees, thought Molly. What were the Pee Wee meetings turning into?

"You'd think he would be on time," grumbled Kevin. "Army guys are always on time."

"Where's our leader, where's our leader!" chanted Kenny. The other Pee Wees joined in and pounded on the table in rhythm. Molly supposed that the only thing worse than having the captain for a Scout leader was having no leader at all.

All of a sudden the door popped open and two people came in. Molly had seen the woman who entered in one of the offices they had passed. The woman had someone with her. The someone was not Captain Spencer. It was a girl not much taller than Rachel, who was the tallest Pee Wee. The girl was chewing bubble gum. Mrs. Peters never liked the Pee Wees to chew gum. The girl must be in the wrong room, thought Molly. Maybe she was a new Pee Wee.

The woman from the office cleared her throat and said, "This is Brandi, and she will be your Scout leader today. Be sure you make her feel welcome."

The woman left quickly as if she was glad to go. Glad not to be a Scout leader herself.

"I'm your new leader," giggled Ms. Bubble Gum. She threw her backpack onto the table, twirled her hair around a finger, blew an enormous purple bubble, and said, "I spell my name with an *i*, not a *y*. I'm a little late because Mrs. Morris kept us after school for wearing makeup to class. There's a rule about that, you know." Brandi rolled her eyes.

The Pee Wees were shocked. Where was Captain Spencer? Molly was beginning to realize there might be worse things than being in the army. And one of them was having a teenage Scout leader! Molly wondered what grade Brandi was in.

"I'm in high school," said Brandi, giggling. "I'm a freshman this year."

"Where's the army guy?" yelled Roger, tipping back in his chair.

"I guess he couldn't handle the job," said Brandi. "He said there were some kids who gave him a hard time. He had to, like, split."

Pop! went another purple bubble.

"So what do you guys do in Scouts?" asked Brandi, sitting down in a chair and tipping it back, just like Roger.

There would be no lining up and marching with this leader, thought Molly. And probably no knot tying.

"We earn badges," said Tracy. "And do good deeds."

Brandi wrinkled up her nose as if she didn't think much of those things.

"We goof off," said Roger. "And go to Playland at the mall. And we order pizzas with lots of pepperoni."

"You're funny," laughed Brandi, pointing her finger at Roger. "I like you."

Roger turned red, but he looked pleased.

No one liked Roger! What was this girl saying?

"How can she think lying is funny?" whispered Mary Beth.

Now that Roger had received attention from their leader, he began to act sillier than ever. He chased Sonny out of the room and down the hall with a rubber spider. A clerk from another office had to bring them back.

"Try to keep your meeting in this room," she said sternly.

"Ta-ta," said Brandi, waving to her with two fingers.

"What does *ta-ta* mean?" Lisa asked Molly.

"I think it's baby talk," Molly said.

"I think it means thanks," said Mary Beth.

Rachel shook her head. "It means good-bye," she said.

Brandi was going through some papers from her backpack. A Pee Wee Scout handbook and a copy of a teen magazine fell out. Brandi paged through the handbook, frowning.

"This stuff looks boring," she said. "When I was in Scouts we did fun stuff like having our colors done and finding out what kind of nail polish stayed on the longest."

Roger groaned.

"I wonder what kind of Scouts she belonged to," said Patty.

"Probably the Fashion Scouts," muttered Kevin.

When no one seemed interested in nail polish and colors, Brandi moved on to other things.

"I think Scouts should learn about dating," she said. "I mean, something practical that we can all use. Stuff they don't teach you in school."

A hush fell over the noisy group. Mary Beth raised her hand. When Brandi didn't respond, she said, "We're only seven. We don't date."

"My mom wouldn't like it if we had to date in Pee Wee Scouts," said Tim.

Molly tried to picture a dating badge. What would be on it? Two people kissing?

"Hey, I'd like that!" said Roger. "All the girls would be lining up to go on a date with me."

Brandi laughed and laughed at Roger's words. "You are so *funny*!" she said.

"That's not funny, it's gross!" said Tracy.

Now Roger was telling his jokes, the same old jokes they had all heard a million times before. But Brandi was roaring at them. "I'd love to take you home with me," she said to Roger as she wiped her eyes. "I could use a cute little brother like you.

"Okay," she said then. "We'll skip the dating badge if it will cause a problem.

Let's think of something else that would be fun."

Mrs. Peters never tried to think of something "fun," thought Molly. She planned ahead and came in and said things like "Today I'm going to tell you about the badge we'll earn next, for skiing." Or for baby-sitting or visiting a nursing home or walking dogs. It was clear that Brandi did not know what she was doing.

"I think I've got it!" Brandi snapped her fingers, showing off her bright blue nail polish. "I'll bet you kids would like to do slimeball art."

CHAPTER 5

One Slimy Mess

"Once when I was in Scouts, a long time ago, we made stuff out of newspaper that had been soaked in water mixed with flour. It got all gooey and slimy and it felt real cool. We shaped it into, like, dolls and spaceships and things. Some kids even made little pretend lipsticks. After it dried, we painted it. Some of it looked really real, like the little red apples and green veggies my friend Bunny made."

Brandi *would* have a friend named Bunny, thought Molly. There was a mixed reaction as the Pee Wees considered Brandi's idea.

"Hey, neat! I'd make a computer, or a robot," said Roger.

"Ms.—I mean Brandi," said Ashley. "I don't think that's a real Scout thing. I mean it isn't helping anyone or anything."

"It sounds like kindergarten," said Rachel.

"I want to make grubworms and snakes," said Sonny. "And maybe a dinosaur or a whale."

"I'll get the stuff, then," said Brandi, standing up and jingling some money around in her pocket. "I've got some supply money here. I'll just run across the street to the store and get what we need. Roger can come with me and help."

After telling the Pee Wees to sit down and think about what they wanted to make, Brandi ran out the door with Roger. He pretended to trip her, and Brandi said, "You little scamp!"

"She didn't even let us vote!" said Jody. "The Pee Wees are supposed to be democratic."

"She didn't pay any attention to what I said," said Ashley.

"She is definitely not a good leader," said Rachel. "Don't you have to go to school or something to be a Scout leader?"

"She's just a substitute," said Tracy. "Maybe there are no classes for that."

Molly felt like pouting. The Pee Wees had been forced into doing Brandi's slimeball project. At least Roger was gone, and Sonny was the only one really acting up. And even he wasn't so bad when he didn't have his partner in crime. Some of the Pee Wees were doing what Brandi had said to do, thinking about what they would make.

But more of them were upset because they had not been asked what they wanted to do. Just forced into doing baby stuff. School stuff. Stuff that didn't help anyone or even earn them a badge.

"She didn't even mention Halloween," grumbled Mary Beth.

"Well, we could make pumpkins out of the gooey paper," said Kenny. "And some witches and spooks."

"It's not the same," said Jody, who rarely complained. "Halloween should be planned. We shouldn't have to think of it ourselves."

"We could leave," said Mary Beth. "And just go home."

Everyone thought about that.

"I think we should go on strike," said Tim. "Like my mom's office did."

"You strike for more money," said Rachel. "We don't get any money from Scouts."

"We could strike to get Mrs. Peters back," said Ashley. "We could say we won't come to the meetings till she comes back."

"I could make those picket signs!" said Tim. "I could cross out the writing on my mom's and write 'Come Back, Mrs. Peters' instead. If any Pee Wees crossed the picket line, they'd be arrested."

Molly was getting nervous. All this talk of striking and quitting scared her. The Pee Wees were about getting along. Strikes and quitting felt like fighting. Not Scout-like at all.

Besides, the Pee Wees were like a family. Quitting would be like getting a divorce. Or having an argument. And Molly hated arguments and fighting and divorce. No, they had to all hang in there together.

"Mrs. Peters is bound to come back soon," said Molly. "Maybe we should make the best of it and pretend this paper stuff is fun."

A few Pee Wees groaned.

"I suppose you're right," said Patty.

"Besides, what would we do on Tuesdays?" said Molly.

Before long, Brandi and Roger were

back. The Pee Wees could hear Roger sliding down the hall and shouting. And they heard Brandi's giggle. They came in carrying flour and pails and lots of old newspapers. Roger had some of the flour in his hair. Molly wondered how he had managed that, when the bag was sealed shut.

"We had to go to my house to get our old newspapers," said Roger.

Brandi didn't waste any time now that they had decided what to do. She sent a few Pee Wees to the rest room to fill the pails with water. Then she dumped in some flour and stirred the gooey mixture with a long spoon.

"I forget if you put anything else in," she said, frowning. "I guess just the newspapers."

Roger and Tim and Sonny tore up paper and tossed it into the pails. Some splashed out and got on the table. And on the floor. And on the boys.

"Yuck!" said Rachel. "My mom isn't going to like me ruining my new jeans. We really need aprons."

"We can be careful," said Brandi, stirring and splashing. She looked as if she was having a better time than the Pee Wees.

"Now!" she said. "Dig in!"

The Pee Wees dug in.

"Is it supposed to be this wet?" asked Ashley. "We can't make stuff out of this!" The water ran down her arms, and the wet newspaper clung to them. *Drip, drip, drip* went the mess onto the floor.

Brandi frowned. "It just needs more flour," she said, adding some.

The mixture was still thin and wet,

but now it had white lumps in it. Big white lumps on the paper.

Jody was trying to make a dog, but the legs fell off in a mushy puddle.

Sonny's grubworm stayed together because it did not have any extra parts.

Soon there was so much flour and water and paper on the floor that the Pee Wees began to slip and slide and fall down.

"Hey, a skating rink! We've got a skating rink here!" shouted Roger.

"I have a feeling we're going to be in trouble," said Mary Beth, who had dried flour on her shirt and face. When the flour dried, it made things stiff.

"A Scout leader is supposed to avoid things like this," said Rachel.

But when they looked at Brandi, she

was helping Roger make a spaceship. She didn't seem to notice the mess in the room. Molly wondered what Brandi's room at home looked like. Did she live in a pigpen?

"This stuff is like really slimy, wet Play-Doh!" said Tracy. "The stuff my little four-year-old brother plays with!"

As Sonny was trying to shape his dinosaur, it slipped from his hands and shot across the table, hitting Roger on the neck.

"Hey!" shouted Roger, turning around. "Quit that!" Then he threw a ball of the slimy dough back at Sonny.

"Hey, a food fight, a food fight!" shouted Tim, joining in. Before long, slimy dough was flying through the air. Now even Brandi wasn't laughing at

Roger. She tried to clap her hands, but they were so wet and slimy they just slid apart without a sound.

And then the door opened, and the mayor walked in. Behind him was Mrs. Stone, Sonny's mother, the assistant Pee Wee Scout leader.

CHAPTER 6

Cleanup Time

Their timing was very bad. Just as they entered the room, Roger threw a ball of slimy dough that missed Sonny and hit the mayor right on the ear. From there it bounced onto Mrs. Stone's pink blouse, leaving a dirty wet ring. The blouse was slippery, and the ball of slime kept sliding down the front of Mrs. Stone until it landed with a plop on one of her suede shoes.

Molly felt as if she were in school and

the principal had come in. But this was even worse than the principal. This was the mayor of the whole town! He probably had the power to lock them all up in the city jail!

Mrs. Stone gave the Pee Wees a hard stare. It was a Mrs. Peters stare. It meant trouble.

"Let's clean up this mess at once," she said. The Pee Wees did. When they were all busy cleaning up and wringing out and wiping off, Mrs. Stone and the mayor asked Brandi to step out into the hall with them. When they returned, Brandi was not with them.

"This room is cleaner now than it was to begin with," said Rachel, wiping up the last of the water on the floor.

"That's because we're all worn out

from work," grumbled Roger. "Look at my hands; they're all rough and red."

"Poor Roger," laughed Mary Beth. "He has dishpan hands!"

When every bit of slimy paper was gone and the room shone, the mayor left. Mrs. Stone explained that it was not the Pee Wees' fault this disaster had occurred.

"I guess we all miss Mrs. Peters," she said.

"Let's write her a letter," said Kevin, "and tell her to come home."

"I'm sure she'll come home as soon as she can," said Mrs. Stone. "But I think she'd love a letter from the Pee Wees."

Sonny's mother passed out paper with lines on it and told them how to spell some words that might give them trouble.

At the top of her paper, Molly wrote in big letters, "PEE WEES FOREVER." Then she wrote, "Come home, Mrs. Peters. We need you a lot."

Molly noticed that Roger was writing about the slimeball meeting. "We couldn't make anything because the paper got all wet and ishy," Molly read.

"I'm going to tell her she's the best Pee Wee leader in the country," said Jody.

"In the world!" said Patty.

"We won't cause any trouble at our meetings if you come back," wrote Molly. "We won't run around or yell or fight and we'll make Roger behave too."

When everyone was finished, Mrs. Stone collected the letters. Sonny's had holes in the paper from erasing. Mrs. Stone put them all into a brown envelope and wrote an address on a label.

"I'll mail this off today," she said. "And now I think it's time for dismissal."

"We didn't have a treat!" yelled Sonny.

"Or talk about good deeds," said Tracy.

"Or sing our song and say our pledge," said Lisa.

"And we didn't talk about a new badge or about a Halloween party," said Kenny.

"I think our meeting was full enough as it was," said their assistant leader. "I for one will be glad to call it a day. I am sure the mayor will be glad to see us leave also."

On the way home, Roger was the only one not feeling low.

"That was embarrassing," said Mary Beth.

"Well, it wasn't our fault," said Ashley.

When Molly got home, her mother met her at the door.

"I heard the news," she said. "Mrs. Stone called me. I'm afraid Brandi won't be back."

Molly didn't know what there was to be afraid about. The only thing to fear was the possibility that Brandi *would* be back! A leader like Brandi was a disaster waiting to happen. Rather, it was a disaster that *had* happened.

"Good," said Molly, noticing in the mirror that her hair was stiff with flour water on one side. "Who will be our leader? Mrs. Stone?"

Her mom shook her head. "Mrs. Stone can't get away every week with those twins at home," she said. "But we'll work it out. Things will turn out for the best."

Molly wondered how her mother knew that. The following Tuesday she found out.

CHAPTER 7

Substitute Leader Number Three

"**I** wonder who will be our leader *this* week," said Ashley on the way to their next meeting.

"Whoever she is, she'll probably be gone by next week," said Patty. "We seem to scare them off."

"Hey, Brandi liked me," said Roger. "It was you guys she couldn't manage."

The Pee Wees got to the town hall and

climbed the broad steps. Molly thought she could see the mayor watching from his window. He was shaking his head and didn't look very happy.

The Pee Wees entered their meeting room, but there was no leader waiting.

"I think we should try to make a very good impression on our new leader when she gets here," said Rachel, throwing her sweater over a chair.

"How can we do that?" asked Sonny.

"By not acting up," Rachel said, glaring at him. "No running around and throwing stuff."

"Hey, I'll bet our new leader will be old and gray, like somebody's grandma," said Roger, pretending to walk with a cane.

But Roger was wrong. The door opened and the new leader walked in.

She was not old or gray, and she did not walk with a cane.

And she was not an army captain or a teenager from the high school.

She was Molly's mother, Mrs. Duff!

Molly did not understand. Her mother should be at work! But perhaps she had taken time off to introduce their new leader.

But no one else followed her, and she took off her jacket and hung it on a hook on the wall. She put some bags she was carrying on the table in the middle of the room. The table that had been full of flour and paper and water only a week ago.

"Good afternoon!" said Mrs. Duff, smiling. "I guess I'm your new Scout leader."

The Pee Wees all clapped and cheered.

Having Mrs. Duff was second best to having Mrs. Peters or Mrs. Stone. But Molly did not clap. Her mother did not belong at Scouts. She belonged at home or at work. And besides, she had not told Molly about this!

"This was a last-minute decision," Mrs. Duff said, looking at Molly. "I couldn't get anyone suitable, so I thought maybe I should do it myself. I found out today that I could leave a little early on Tuesdays by working during my lunch hour. And I said, Why not? So here I am! I hope I can run the ship until Mrs. Peters returns, so that you don't have any more changes. We can get right down to business and earn some badges now."

Everyone cheered again. This certainly sounded good. To everyone but

Molly. How could she surprise her family with new badges if her mother was the one who was handing them out?

And who wanted to have their mom in charge of things at home *and* at Scout meetings? The last time Molly had felt like this was when her parents had come along with Mr. and Mrs. Peters and all the Pee Wees on their trip to the Science and History Museum in Center City. Molly had dreaded it, but it had turned out all right. The Pee Wees had all liked her parents and thought her dad was very funny.

Would she be lucky again, or would this whole leader thing be a disaster?

"Hey, isn't this great?" whispered Mary Beth to Molly. "Why didn't you tell us your mom was going to be our new leader?"

"I didn't know," said Molly.

"We're really lucky," said Jody. "Your mom will be a great leader."

If Jody thought it was great, Molly felt better about the whole thing. Molly liked Jody. He was smart and he was kind. After all, it wasn't the most important thing in the world to surprise your parents with badges.

Mrs. Duff started the meeting the right way, by singing the Pee Wee song, saying the Pee Wee pledge, and hearing about all their good deeds.

The good deeds had been piling up for three weeks because no one had asked to hear them in all that time.

"I've got piles of good deeds," said Tim.

"I've got tons of them," said Sonny.

"I've got three weeks' worth of good deeds," said Tracy.

"I didn't do any because Mrs. Peters wasn't here," said Roger. "Why waste time doing good deeds when there's no one to tell about them?"

The Pee Wees booed Roger, and Mrs. Duff explained that the reason for doing good deeds was to help others, not just to tell about them.

"I still think it's a waste," said Roger. "I'll do some new ones this week."

The other Pee Wees told about their good deeds. Lots of them had walked dogs and cleaned their rooms. Three weeks of good deeds took quite a while to tell, but at last they were through.

"Now I think we'll learn a few new exercises," said their leader, "so that we won't get restless and bother the mayor with our energy."

First she showed them bending and stretching exercises. Then some swinging windmill exercises. And finally, some make-believe bicycle-riding exercises.

"Wow," said Roger. "I'm pooped!"

Rachel frowned at Roger. "Can't you say *tired* like anyone else?" she said.

Roger stuck his tongue out at Rachel.

"And now," said Molly's mother, "I have a treat for all of you."

The Pee Wees cheered. This was what a real meeting was all about. Good deeds and treats. Especially treats. Things were back to normal at last.

Mrs. Duff reached into one bag and took out some paper plates with fall leaves on them. Then she took out some paper cups with pumpkins on them!

"Your mom hasn't forgotten about Halloween!" said Mary Beth. "That's a good sign!"

From the other bag, Mrs. Duff took out some fudge bars with candy corn stuck in the top. And a big Thermos of milk. And last of all, some big, shiny red apples.

"Roger and Tim, would you help pass these out?" she said.

Roger was surprised to be asked to help. Molly was surprised too. Her mom knew how to treat Roger. She gave him some attention before he even had a chance to act up. Mothers can be smart sometimes, thought Molly.

"And when we finish eating," said Mrs. Duff, "I have some news. Some good Pee Wee news."

CHAPTER 8

Mrs. Duff Saves the Day

Her mom just did another smart thing, Molly realized. To make sure they didn't play with their food or start a food fight, she told them about the good news beforehand. They knew that the sooner they had eaten and cleaned up, the sooner they would hear it. It was good to see her mother in action.

Sure enough, it worked just the way Molly thought it would. No one played with their food. They ate it and enjoyed it, then washed up and waited to hear the news.

"I think the first thing we should plan is a Halloween party," said their substitute leader.

"Rah, rah, rah!" shouted the Pee Wees. A good leader knew what they wanted to hear, thought Molly.

"It's always nice to mix fun with helping someone, don't you think?" were Mrs. Duff's next words.

The Pee Wees groaned. Was this going to be another one of those parties in a nursing home or a hospital? Although they all had to admit that both of those parties had turned out to be fun.

"What about a party that's just fun and nothing else?" said Sonny.

Mrs. Duff laughed, although Molly

did not think what Sonny had said was very funny.

"It's more fun when you know you're doing something worthwhile," said Mrs. Duff.

Sonny and Roger were shaking their heads as if they did not agree with that.

"What about if we have fun, help others, and earn a badge at the same time?" their new leader asked.

Mention of a new badge got everyone's attention. They all agreed that at least two of those three things went well together.

"Your mom is as good a leader as Mrs. Peters!" said Kevin.

"She's more like Mrs. Peters than Mrs. Peters!" said Rachel.

"I thought we would turn the tables

on Halloween this year," said Mrs. Duff. "Every year we do the same thing, go house to house and ask for something for ourselves."

"What's the matter with that?" shouted Roger.

"That's what Halloween is for," said Sonny.

"Yes, but it could be time for a change," said Mrs. Duff. "What if we turn it around and *give* something instead of *take* something?"

"Oh, like a backward Halloween!" said Ashley.

"And we could get a backward badge!" said Kevin.

"We could wear it with the wrong side out!" said Jody. "Cool."

"Dumb," said Sonny. "I want my candy!"

"How do we have a backward Halloween?" asked Mary Beth with a frown.

"Well," said their leader, "we will still dress up and go trick-or-treating. But instead of taking candy, we'll give *them* candy! Or something nice. It doesn't have to be candy. There are a lot of people who live alone in our neighborhood, who are lonely and don't see children often. Think what a treat it would be if we visited them and brought them something special. Like a nice warm dinner, or a homemade pumpkin pie, or even a pair of warm slippers for these cold nights."

"I can't bake a homemade pie, Mrs. Duff," said Patty. "My mom won't let me use the oven alone."

"But your mom may want to donate a

homemade pie, Patty, and you could deliver it."

"You mean we give out a pie at every single house?" asked Tim.

"How do we know who to go to?" asked Tracy.

"We won't go to every house in the neighborhood. I thought each of you could choose one person to visit. Altogether that will be thirteen stops. We will all go together as a group. Talk this over with your parents and choose someone you think would like a surprise. Afterward we'll come to our house for hot cocoa and treats and games. That way we'll have our party, do something nice for others, and get our badge for being Halloween helpers. How does that sound?"

Most of the Pee Wees cheered. But a few of them frowned.

"After the thirteen backward things, can we do regular trick-or-treating?" asked Tim.

"If it isn't too late," said their leader. "And it isn't too cold."

The Pee Wees were won over. No one could resist regular trick-or-treating and a party and a badge.

Everyone began to talk at once, telling Mrs. Duff whose houses they wanted to go to.

"There's a man who lives by me who has no teeth," said Roger. "But I think he could chew pumpkin pie. No one ever goes to see him because he's so grumpy."

"He sounds like he might need a

friend to bring him a gift," said Mrs. Duff. "If he will let us in. We have to remember to only go where we are wanted. We don't want to force ourselves on anyone."

"I think we should take a treat to Brandi," said Roger. "She liked me."

"Then you take her a treat yourself, White," said Kenny.

"Roger may have a good idea," said Mrs. Duff thoughtfully. "It would be a chance to show Brandi there are no hard feelings. That we appreciate her trying to help us out."

Then she added, "I'll bet the captain would like a treat too. I'll put him on our list as my choice." Mrs. Duff got a notebook from her bag and wrote Captain Spencer's name down.

"That will make it fourteen sur-
prises," said Lisa.

"Once we have their names and inter-
ests, let's think about what kind of treat
would be best for each person. We want
to choose something they will really like.
We wouldn't want to give someone a
musical CD, for example, if they don't
like to listen to music. I'll get in touch
with your parents later and we'll make
more plans."

For the rest of the meeting the Pee
Wees talked about what they were going
to wear for the backward Halloween.

"I think we should put our costumes
on backward!" said Kevin.

"Or inside out," said Lisa.

"Are we going to say 'Trick or treat'
backward at their door?" asked Ashley.

Rachel got out a paper and wrote

something down. "That would be 'taert ro kcirt!' " she said. "It doesn't make any sense!"

"Then we can walk backward instead!" said Kevin. "Jody can wheel his chair backward too!"

Mrs. Duff laughed. "You see," she said, "doing the opposite thing will make this Halloween more fun than ever!"

"No one else will have a Halloween like it!" said Tracy. "We'll be the only ones who do things backward, upside down, and inside out."

CHAPTER 9

The Backward Halloween

The Pee Wees liked to be different. They liked to be unusual. And this Halloween was going to be just that.

Molly was used to rushing home from the Scout meeting to tell her mom all the news. But she couldn't do that today. Her mom already knew the news! Her mom had told *them* the news! Instead of going home to tell her, Molly went home *with* her. And they both told Mr. Duff about the backward Halloween at supper.

"Can I come?" asked Mr. Duff. Molly laughed, but Mrs. Duff said, "That's not a bad idea. I need parents to help, and you're a parent."

All week the Pee Wees thought about Halloween. They mostly thought about what they would wear. On Saturday Molly and Mary Beth walked to the center of town to look in stores.

"We can just get ideas," said Molly, "and then we can go home and make the costumes ourselves."

Mary Beth nodded. "My mom says homemade costumes are best."

Molly didn't think so. But homemade things were cheaper, and she liked to save her parents money. Besides, costumes were fun to make.

Most of the stores had window displays of scary Halloween costumes. The girls stopped in front of one window that showed a dragon costume.

"I don't want to be a boring animal or a witch or ghost," said Molly. "Let's be something no one else will think of."

"Like what?" asked Mary Beth.

"Like a computer with legs," said Molly. "Or a stalk of celery."

"That isn't scary," said her friend. "And it would be hard to make."

"How about a candy bar?" said Molly. "It wouldn't be scary, but no one else would be one. And it would be easy to make. Just some brown paper with words on it, and holes for eyes."

"I could be a Nut Crunchy!" said Mary Beth, "With red and green paper. And you could be a Chocolate Delight!"

"Let's do it!" said Molly.

Just as the girls were leaving, Roger and Sonny came up behind them.

"Boo!" said Roger. "Hey, I'm getting that dragon costume, and Sonny is getting the Spider-Man outfit."

"We're making ours," said Mary Beth.

"My dad has a lot of money," bragged Roger. "I can get the most expensive one in the store."

"I'm going to wear Spider-Man backward," said Sonny. "You know, for the backward Halloween."

"Sonny *is* backward," said Mary Beth. "He doesn't need to prove it with his costume."

On the way home, Molly said, "No one could tell if ours were backward or not. They're the same either way!"

"We don't want to be like Sonny anyway," said Mary Beth.

All the Pee Wees worked on their costumes during the week. On Tuesday they met and talked about the people they had chosen to visit on Halloween.

Hands waved. "Mrs. Duff, there's a lady in the apartment house near us who has no children or relatives," said Rachel. "My mom says she likes to play cards, but she has no one to play with. So our treat is going to be to go there once a week and play cards with her."

"What a wonderful idea for a treat, Rachel!" said Mrs. Duff.

"Mrs. Duff," said Patty, waving her hand. "We chose the foreign student who lives with the family next door. She doesn't know many people here, and she loves American movies. We're getting her a video of one of the old musicals. From Kenny and me."

"Hey, you could run it backward, for the backward Halloween," said Tim.

"It won't be Halloween when she watches it," said Rachel.

"What creative Pee Wees!" said Mrs. Duff. "That's just what I hoped you'd do, think of something special to do for someone."

More hands waved, and more ideas were announced. Ideas for mittens and scarves and cookies and pies and TV dinners. Ideas for helping in the yard and dusting and carrying in groceries.

"These sound like good deeds," grumbled Sonny. "Not like Halloween stuff. It sounds like work."

"He's so lazy," said Ashley. "And selfish."

"What a baby," said Lisa.

Molly felt sorry for Sonny. He was spoiled, but he could be nice sometimes too.

After Mrs. Duff was sure everyone knew what treat they were bringing on Halloween, and whom they were bringing it to, the Pee Wees worked on their costumes. The ones who had bought theirs, or already had them finished, helped the others who were making their own. Soon the room was filled with colorful goblins and pumpkins and crayons and paper and glue. Mrs. Duff played some scary Halloween music and passed out pumpkin cookies. The afternoon flew past. By the time they cleaned up and got ready to leave, it was getting dark.

"Whoooooooooo," hooted Tim. "I'm a Halloween owl!"

"It gets dark so early now," said Kevin.

"All the better to haunt you with!" said Jody. He had paper pumpkins taped all over his wheelchair.

"Well, I think we're all ready for the big day," said Mrs. Duff.

"The big backward day!" cried the Pee Wees.

CHAPTER 10

Tricks or Treats, Pee Wee Style

On Halloween night, the Pee Wees were ready. The two candy bars met the dragon and ghosts and goblins at the town hall. Even Mr. and Mrs. Duff had costumes on. They were dressed as Dracula and his wife. Everyone carried a big bag, but it was not for collecting treats. It was for giving them out.

"We have to go to my person's house first," said Tracy, "because my treat is a

96

dinner for Mr. and Mrs. Matson, and they have to eat it while it's hot."

When the Pee Wees got to their first stop, the Matsons were expecting them.

"Your mom called," they said. "What a wonderful treat! A home-cooked dinner for two! We saved our appetites all afternoon!"

Tracy took the dinners out of her bag. They smelled good, thought Molly. The Matsons gave Tracy a big hug and thanked her over and over again. Then they gave each Pee Wee a fat caramel apple.

As they left, Tracy said, "This is more fun than asking for stuff."

Molly agreed. It gave her a nice warm feeling to help someone and give gifts.

"Look at all those kids," said Sonny, pointing his Spider-Man finger across the street. "They're all asking for stuff, instead of sharing."

Mary Beth laughed. "This is the first time Sonny shared anything, and now he thinks everyone else is greedy!"

The Pee Wees went from house to house, making people happy with warm mittens, scarves, home-canned fruit, and promises of yardwork and household help and games of cards. One man even had tears in his eyes.

"No one ever did this for me before," he said. "It's like Christmas."

"I think we should do this more often," said Jody. "It's so much fun!"

Everyone agreed. It was fun to share.

"Here's where the mean guy lives,"

said Roger. "I've got a pie for him, but I don't want to ring the bell. He might throw a pumpkin at me."

The grumpy man opened the door. "Go away," he said. "I don't have any candy to give out."

"But we brought *you* something," said Mr. Duff. "Roger has a homemade pumpkin pie for you."

"I can't chew anything," said the man. "I have no teeth."

"You don't need teeth," said Lisa bravely. "Pumpkin pie is soft. My baby sister can eat it, and she's only a year old."

"Soft, is it?" said the man. "Well, hand it over then."

The man took the pie and slammed the door.

Roger made a fist at the closed door. "See, I told you! He's mean!"

"People are all different," laughed Mrs. Duff. "He may have lots of problems and no family to love him. That's the kind of person who needs a treat the most."

"I still think he could have said thank you," said Kevin.

The next stop was Brandi's house. Brandi answered the door. Her hair was dyed green.

"Hey, you guys!" she said, snapping her purple gum. "It's good to see you again! I'll bet Sonny is Spider-Man, and ho ho, that's my friend Roger in the dragon suit!"

"We just wanted to say happy Halloween and thank you for helping us out that Tuesday," said Mrs. Duff, handing Brandi a small package.

"Well, I guess Scout leading isn't my thing," said Brandi.

"That's for sure," whispered Molly to Mary Beth. She was thinking of the flour, water, and newspaper mixture.

"I'm not too good at things I do with my hands." Brandi opened the package and said, "Hey, thanks, you guys! I've been wanting one of these little lighted makeup mirrors!"

"It's for your purse," said Ashley. "My aunt has one."

Molly wasn't sure Brandi had a purse, but she could probably use the mirror anyway.

After Brandi gave them each a hug, the Pee Wees left.

"Maybe now she won't put on so

much makeup," said Sonny. "She probably couldn't see what she was doing."

"Now our last stop," said Mr. Duff.
"The captain's house."

When the captain came to the door, he
was dressed in an army uniform.

"Hey, he really *is* a soldier!" said
Kevin.

"Well, if it isn't the Pee Wee Scouts,"
he said. "Fall in, all of you."

The Pee Wees fell in. Into his living
room.

"Are you in the army?" asked Tim.

"Not anymore," said the captain,
clicking his heels together. "I just got out
my old uniform and dusted it off for a
Halloween party tonight."

He gave the Pee Wees each a candy
bar.

"Hey, a Chocolate Delight for a Chocolate Delight," said Jody to Molly.

"They're my favorite," said Molly.

"Mine too," said Jody.

Did Jody mean the candy, or me? wondered Molly. Either way, they had something in common.

"We brought you some warm socks," said Molly. "My grandma knit them."

"Why, thank you," said the captain. "Look, they match my uniform. I'll put them on right now. They're not regulation, of course, but no one will notice."

The captain began to tell them old war stories, but Mrs. Duff had to cut him short because of time.

"We have miles to go before we sleep," said Mr. Duff, quoting from a poem that Molly knew was his favorite.

They didn't really have to go miles. Just blocks.

"Ready, *march!*" said the captain, opening the front door. And march they did, right down the steps and down the block.

"Now!" said Sonny. "We get to go regular trick-or-treating!"

"Just on this block, where we can see you," said Mrs. Duff.

The Pee Wees dashed off, shouting, "trick or treat!" They came back with even more candy bars.

On the way to the Duffs', Rachel said, "It really was more fun taking treats to people instead of getting them."

All the Pee Wees agreed, even though Roger and Sonny pretended they didn't.

CHAPTER 11

Badges for All

"As soon as we get in, I'd like to take a group photo of everyone in their costumes," said Mr. Duff. "We want to remember this backward Halloween for years to come."

Everyone walked a little faster, thinking of the party that awaited them. Roger and Sonny began to race. "Last one there's a rotten pumpkin!" yelled Roger. A few of the other boys joined in the race. Roger, who had trouble with his long dragon's tail, could not move very fast. When he saw that he was falling behind, he gave Sonny a shove. Sonny shoved him back, and Roger tripped on his tail and fell right into the only big mud puddle on the sidewalk!

Mud splattered everywhere, but most of it was on Roger. The green dragon turned brown, and the dragon's face looked very, very angry. Roger caught Sonny and tried to push him in the puddle too.

"Boys!" said Mrs. Duff in her Scout leader's voice. "That's enough!"

And it was enough, thought Molly. Enough to soak Roger to his underwear. When they got to the Duffs', Mrs. Duff had to help him off with his costume and into an old pink bathrobe of

Molly's. Roger turned bright red. "I can't wear this!" he said.

"It's all we have right now," said Mrs. Duff. "You can't stay in those wet clothes for the whole party."

Everyone tried not to laugh, except Sonny, and even though Roger was in the back row of the picture, the pink bathrobe with the lace collar showed up very well.

"Just think of it as another costume, Roger," said Mr. Duff. "You're at the party dressed as a Barbie doll."

"Hey, yeah, that's what I am!" said Roger, prancing around to show off.

After the picture, the Pee Wees bobbed for apples and played games. Mr. Duff told scary stories with the lights out and only one candle lit. At the end of the evening Mrs. Duff said,

"Now it's time for the Backward Halloween badges!" She gave them out, saying, "You've all been good Halloween helpers."

Molly pinned her badge on her shirt with all her other badges. The more badges the better, she thought. Molly guessed that was true of many things. It was fun to collect things. Especially badges, because they meant something special.

The Duffs brought out hot dogs and buns, baked beans, and batwing cookies. There was apple cider to drink. Molly noticed that all the chairs were at the table backward! When had her dad done that?

"I think," said Mrs. Duff when everyone had turned their chair around, "that we'll start with dessert tonight."

The Pee Wees looked surprised. They all liked dessert best.

"Oh, I know!" said Ashley. "It's a backward meal for a backward Halloween!"

"That's right," said their leader.

While they were eating, Mrs. Duff made an announcement.

"I'm glad to be able to tell you some good news," she said. "I have a letter here to all the Pee Wees from Mrs. Peters. She said she loved your letters, and that her mother is better. She's coming home next week."

The Pee Wees cheered.

"But you were just as good a leader as Mrs. Peters," said Mary Beth to Molly's mother. The rest of the Pee Wees agreed.

"I enjoyed it," said Mrs. Duff.

"I think we should end by giving a

prize for the best costume," said Mr. Duff. "Molly's mother and I will be the judges."

Molly's parents put their heads together and talked in low tones. Then Mr. Duff said, "There are wonderful costumes here tonight, but we both agreed that one of the costumes stands out over all the rest. The best costume prize goes to—Roger White, the Barbie doll!"

Roger stood up in the pink bathrobe and came to collect his prize—a pink hair ribbon to match the robe!

Roger put it on, and Mr. Duff said, "You're a good sport, Roger! And that's what is important to learn in Scouts—how to be a good sport!"

Roger bowed and did a little dance, and everyone laughed and clapped.

"He's not really a good sport," said

Rachel. "He just likes the attention—even when he looks silly."

Before Mr. Duff drove the Pee Wees home, they all stood in a big circle and held hands. They sang the Pee Wee song and said the Pee Wee pledge.

The backward Halloween was over. It had been a big success, thought Molly. Even though their real leader was gone, her mom had saved the day, rescuing them from Brandi and the captain. They had helped others, had fun, and gotten their badges. Next week they would see Mrs. Peters again, and baby Nick, and meet in Mrs. Peters's basement where they belonged.

Rat's knees, what more could a Pee Wee Scout ask for?

Pee Wee Scout Song
(to the tune of
"Old MacDonald Had a Farm")

Scouts are helpers, Scouts have fun
Pee Wee, Pee Wee Scouts!
We sing and play when work is done,
Pee Wee, Pee Wee Scouts!

With a good deed here,
And an errand there,
Here a hand, there a hand,
Everywhere a good hand.

Scouts are helpers, Scouts have fun,
Pee Wee, Pee Wee Scouts!

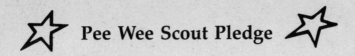 **Pee Wee Scout Pledge**

We love our country
And our home,
Our school and neighbors too.

As Pee Wee Scouts
We pledge our best
In everything we do.